Top D●gs

I Love My Golden Retriever

Abigail Beal

PowerKiDS press
New York

This book is dedicated to you and your pet— a special friendship based on loyalty, respect, and kindness.

Published in 2011 by The Rosen Publishing Group, Inc.
29 East 21st Street, New York, NY 10010

First Edition

Editor: Joanne Randolph
Book Design: Greg Tucker

Photo Credits: Cover Goodshoot/Thinkstock; pp. 4, 5, 8, 9, 10, 11, 14–15 (main), 15 (right), 16–17 (main), 17 (right), 18–19, 20, 21, 22 Shutterstock.com; p. 6 Douglas Miller/Getty Images; p. 7 Stephen Chernin/Getty Images; pp. 12–13 iStockphoto/Thinkstock; p. 13 (right) Janie Airey/Lifesize/Thinkstock; p. 14 (left) Ghislain & Marie David de Lossy/Getty Images; p. 16 (left) © McPHOTO/age fotostock.

Library of Congress Cataloging-in-Publication Data

Beal, Abigail.
I love my golden retriever / by Abigail Beal. — 1st ed.
    p. cm. — (Top dogs)
Includes index.
ISBN 978-1-4488-2536-3 (library binding) — ISBN 978-1-4488-2656-8 (pbk.) —
ISBN 978-1-4488-2657-5 (6-pack)
1. Golden retriever—Juvenile literature. I. Title.
SF429.G63B43 2011
636.752′7—dc22
                                        2010022369

Manufactured in the United States of America

CPSIA Compliance Information: Batch #WW11PK: For Further Information contact Rosen Publishing, New York, New York at 1-800-237-9932

Contents

Meet the Golden Retriever

Golden retrievers, sometimes called goldens, are very **popular** dogs. It is easy to see why. Many people pick golden retrievers for their friendly faces and happy **personalities**. Golden retrievers are known for being easy to train and smart. This means your golden retriever wants to learn commands. Even as young

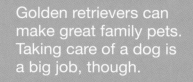

Golden retrievers can make great family pets. Taking care of a dog is a big job, though.

puppies, these dogs want to be their owners' friends and work hard as service animals.

The golden retriever is a dog anyone would love, but not every family should get one. This dog needs lots of space to play and be active both indoors and outside. Do you want to find out more about golden retrievers?

Have you seen a dog that looks like this one before? If so, you have seen a golden retriever!

The golden retriever was first **bred** to retrieve waterfowl for hunters. Today you will find golden retrievers playing with their families or hunting. Their **ancestry** begins with the breeding of two yellow retrievers. Other breeds were added to the mix over time to bring us today's golden retrievers. Sir Dudley Marjoribanks, first Lord Tweedmouth of Scotland, was

This golden sits with its owner at a dog show in England in the 1930s.

the first breeder of golden retrievers in the early 1800s.

   In the late 1800s, British **immigrants** brought golden retrievers to North America. The American Kennel Club first accepted the dogs as a breed in 1925. Samuel S. Magoffin, an American sportsman, began the Golden Retriever Club of America in 1938.

This golden is being judged at a dog show in the United States. The judges will pick the dog that is closest to the breed standard as the winner.

What Do Golden Retrievers Look Like?

How do you know if a dog is a golden retriever? Look for its long, golden coat of fur, which gives the breed its name. The fur on its body is longer around the bottom and at the back of its legs. A golden retriever also has a long tail with feathered fur underneath it. The ears of a golden retriever are short and fold neatly. Its eyes are large

Golden retrievers can have fur that is very light. They can also have darker, almost orange fur, as this golden does.

Here you can see the longer fur on this golden retriever's chest, belly, and tail.

and dark brown and seem to show its warm, friendly personality.

Golden retrievers are medium-sized dogs. They generally weigh between 55 and 75 pounds (25–34 kg). They can be from 21.5 to 24 inches (55–61 cm) tall at the tops of their shoulders. Goldens are just a bit longer than they are tall.

Strong and Athletic

The golden retriever is bred as a hunting dog. They find and carry hunted **game** in their mouths. The golden retriever must be gentle with its catch. Hunters do not want their dogs to eat the game or put holes in its body with their teeth. They are also bred for entering the water to retrieve game. Their coats are thick and **water-repellent**.

Many golden retrievers love to play catch with a tennis ball or other toy. Running after the ball and jumping to catch it is great exercise for your pet.

Golden retrievers are strong and **athletic**. They enjoy outdoor activities. Because they were bred as retrievers of water birds, golden retrievers that are family pets often enjoy playing catch, carrying objects in their mouths, and swimming.

This golden retriever is bringing a game bird back to its owner. Some owners pick goldens for their natural skill as retrievers.

Smart and Friendly

The golden retriever can be a wonderful pet for a family. This dog is **intelligent** and easy to train. If owners treat their goldens with **respect** and kindness, they will find themselves with some **devoted** pets!

Golden retrievers can be great pets, but they are not for everyone. Athletic golden retrievers need plenty of room to play and exercise. The golden retriever is friendly

Golden retrievers love being with their families. Children in a family can help give a golden the exercise it needs by taking it for walks.

and has lots of energy. As it is checking out things in your home, its long tail can easily sweep things off a low table. Golden retrievers are not trying to cause trouble, they are just curious!

Golden retrievers like to be active, but they need quiet time, too. This golden is taking a rest on the couch.

Taking Care of Your Golden

Taking care of your golden retriever is important. This will help your golden retriever lead a long and healthy life with you. Feeding your golden retriever healthy food throughout its life will help it be strong and full of energy. Your pet also needs clean water at all times.

Many people like the golden retriever's thick, soft coat. However,

You will need to buy a special brush to care for your golden retriever's fur.

Golden retrievers will need a bath every few months. You may have to bathe your pet more often if it gets extra dirty.

a golden's owner must brush his pet's coat at least two times a week. Every owner should microchip her dog and keep an identification tag on her dog's collar. This will help people return your pet should it get lost. Regular visits to the veterinarian are important, too.

Your golden puppy will need to wear a collar that fits. The collar should be loose enough to fit two fingers between it and the dog's neck.

Training a Golden Retriever

As does any dog, golden retrievers need training. The best way to train your golden retriever is by using praise and healthy treats. People train dogs so the dogs can learn what we expect from them. Training builds a **relationship** of trust with your pet. Golden retrievers are smart. They enjoy learning

This golden retriever is being trained as a rescue dog. It takes a lot of training to get a dog ready for this important job.

You will first train your golden to come, sit, stay, and lie down. This golden is being taught to "shake," or give its paw to its owner.

new skills and they want to make their owners happy. This makes them easy to train.

A training class can be a good place to learn the basics. You can learn harder skills there, too. Training gives you a way to communicate, or talk, with your furry friend. As with learning any new language, it may take practice. It will be worth it, though!

Because of their breeding, many goldens like to have something in their mouths. You will need to teach your golden retriever puppy what things it can chew on.

Golden Retrievers at Work

The golden retriever is gentle and easy to work with. Because of this, goldens are often used to do important jobs. You will find golden retrievers working to help the elderly. They often work as service dogs helping the blind or other people with disabilities. They are also used as **therapy** dogs. Goldens have been used to help children with

autism connect better with those around them. They are even used to help children learn to read.

If you are looking for a guard dog, you may want to pick another breed. That said, golden retrievers have been used in police work because they have keen senses.

This golden retriever is working as a guide dog for a blind person. Many service dogs wear special harnesses, as this dog does, to let people know they are working.

Is a Golden Right for You?

Most people who own golden retrievers love them! This may be true for your family, too. However, it is important to think about what this dog needs before you get one. Do you have enough space and time to keep your active pet healthy and happy? If you do not have a lot of time for walks or playing games of catch, this may

not be the right breed for you. A bored dog often finds ways to get into trouble. Keeping your golden busy will make everybody happier.

If you are looking for a fun, friendly pet to do things with your family, then a golden might be just right! If you do get a golden, have fun with your new pet!

Golden retrievers that get plenty of walks and playtime, as these two dogs do, make better family pets.

Golden Retriever Facts

1. Buddy, Eagle, and Chance were golden retrievers that appeared in *Air Bud*. Duke is a golden in Bush's Baked Beans ads.

2. Some famous people have owned golden retrievers. President Gerald Ford's golden was named Liberty. Oprah Winfrey has three golden retrievers, Luke, Layla, and Gracie.

3. Golden retrievers became popular in the United States starting in 1940.

4. People once thought golden retrievers were descended, or came from, Russian circus dogs.

5. Golden retrievers are often used as search and rescue dogs, which find people buried under fallen buildings or other places.

6. The golden retriever is the second most popular sporting and pet dog in the United States. The Labrador retriever is the most popular.

22

Glossary

ancestry (AN-ses-tree) Having to do with relatives that lived long ago.

athletic (ath-LEH-tik) Having a strong, fit body that can do lots of exercise and activities.

autism (AW-tih-zum) A set of problems some people have that may include trouble dealing with others or talking.

bred (BRED) To have brought a male and a female animal together so they will have babies.

devoted (dih-VOHT-ed) Gave effort, attention, and time to a purpose.

game (GAYM) Wild animals that are hunted for food.

immigrants (IH-muh-grunts) People who move to a new country from another country.

intelligent (in-TEH-luh-jent) Smart.

personalities (per-sun-A-lih-teez) How people or animals act with others.

popular (PAH-pyuh-lur) Liked by lots of people.

relationship (rih-LAY-shun-ship) A connection, generally with friends and family.

respect (rih-SPEKT) To think highly of someone or something.

therapy (THER-uh-pee) Something done to help a person figure out his feelings.

water-repellent (waw-ter-rih-PEH-lent) Keeps water away.

Index

Web Sites

Due to the changing nature of Internet links, PowerKids Press has developed an online list of Web sites related to the subject of this book. This site is updated regularly. Please use this link to access the list: www.powerkidslinks.com/topd/goldenr/